DOUBLE-RHYME

Does Anyone Have a Spare Bear?

by Dick Punnett
illustrated by
Helen Endres

THE
CHILD'S
WORLD

MANKATO, MN 56001

To Don and Helen,
who have had every pet EXCEPT a bear!

Library of Congress Cataloging in Publication Data

Punnett, Richard Douglas.
  Does anyone have a spare bear?

  (Double-rhyme books)
  Summary: A lonely bear in a village fair finds
happiness at last with a spare bear from Delaware.
    1. Children's stories, American.   [1. Bears—Fiction.
2. Stories in rhyme]   I. Endres, Helen.   II. Title.
III. Series.
PZ8.3.P97DO   1985   [E]   84-23009
ISBN 0-89565-304-4

DOUBLE~RHYME

Does Anyone Have a Spare Bear?

Our village has a fair where…

we keep a lonely rare bear.

He sits upon a square chair...

sunk in deep despair there.

I watched his lonely bear stare...

and cried, "We need a pair there!"

I looked with very rare care,

searching EVERYWHERE there,

but no one had a spare bear.

So I paid a special air fare…

16

and flew to Delaware where...

I knew there was a bear lair.

But when I felt some bear hair...

and saw a mean BEWARE glare,

I got an awful scare there!

So I said my special bear prayer,

then shot my super air flare...

--just the perfect bear scare--

and caught her in my square snare!

So now she's in the fair where…

they make a happy pair there.

About the Author:

Dick Punnett grew up in Penfield, New York, and graduated from Principia College in Elsah, Illinois. After further studies at the Art Center School and Chouinard Art Institute in Los Angeles, he became a writer-cartoonist for a Hollywood animation studio. His current residence is in Ormond Beach, Florida, where he and his wife live along the Tomoka River. Mr. Punnett is the author of the popular Talk-Along books.

About the Artist:

Helen Endres is a commercial artist, designer and illustrator of children's books. She has lived and worked in the Chicago area since coming from her native Oklahoma in 1952. Graduated from Tulsa University with a BA, she received further training at Hallmark in Kansas City and from the Chicago Art Institute. Ms. Endres attributes much of her creative achievement to the advice and encouragement of her Chicago contemporaries and to the good humor and patience of the hundreds of young models who have posed for her.